g	B
f	G
b	F
u	L
o	U
l	O

Flop is Brett's dragon.

Flop has black skin and pink spots.

A dragon
is a fun pet!
Flop nods.

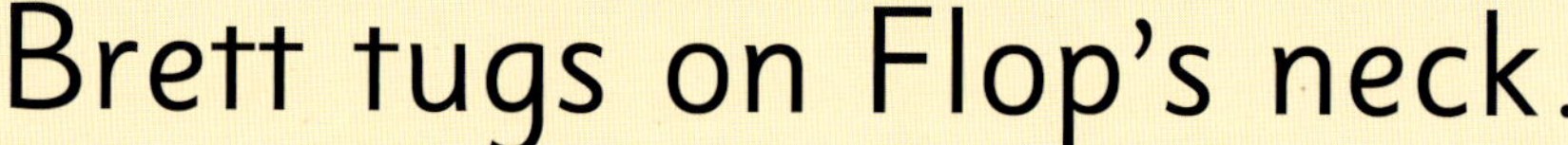

Up, up!

But Flop cannot.

Brett and Flop drop.

Brett grips on and gulps.

Bump! Flop and Brett land on a daffodil.

Flop is upset.

Brett hugs Flop.

Flop hiccups...
Hic!
...and pop!

A dragon's egg! Flop is a mom!